W9-AJU-537

TEAM PLAY? FORGET IT!

Brian and Will were freezing her out!

Jo couldn't believe it. After all those games when she'd led the Bulls in assists! *Man,* Jo thought, *for one game I concentrate on my own scoring, and what happens? My "loyal" teammates freeze me out. Well, if* that's *how it's gonna be . . .*

For the next ten minutes Jo put up shots each time she got her hands on the ball. She took layups, jumpers, and running one-handers from every angle. Sometimes she was open, sometimes there were three defenders draped over her.

It didn't matter. She just kept shooting.

Don't miss any of the books in

—a slammin', jammin', in-your-face action series from Bantam Books!

#1 Crashing the Boards

#2 In Your Face!

#3 Trash Talk

#4 Monster Jam

#5 One on One

#6 Show Time!

#7 Slam Dunk!

Coming soon:

#9 Hang Time

BALL HOG

by

Hank Herman

BANTAM BOOKS
NEW YORK • TORONTO • LONDON • SYDNEY • AUCKLAND

RL 2.6, 007-010

BALL HOG

A Bantam Book / December 1996

*Produced by Daniel Weiss Associates, Inc.
33 West 17th Street
New York, NY 10011.*

Cover art by Jeff Mangiat.

All rights reserved.

*Copyright © 1996 by Daniel Weiss Associates, Inc., and
Hank Herman.*

*Cover art copyright © 1996 by Daniel Weiss Associates, Inc.
No part of this book may be reproduced or transmitted
in any form or by any means, electronic or mechanical,
including photocopying, recording, or by any information
storage and retrieval system, without permission in
writing from the publisher.
For information address: Bantam Books.*

If you purchased this book without a cover you should be aware that this book is stolen property. It was reported as "unsold and destroyed" to the publisher and neither the author nor the publisher has received any payment for this "stripped book."

ISBN: 0-553-48430-3

Published simultaneously in the United States and Canada

Bantam Books are published by Bantam Books, a division of Bantam Doubleday Dell Publishing Group, Inc. Its trademark, consisting of the words "Bantam Books" and the portrayal of a rooster, is Registered in U.S. Patent and Trademark Office and in other countries. Marca Registrada. Bantam Books, 1540 Broadway, New York, New York 10036.

PRINTED IN THE UNITED STATES OF AMERICA

OPM 0 9 8 7 6 5 4 3 2 1

To Matt, an athlete for all seasons

Jo Meyerson tried to back her brother in under the basket, but it wasn't working. At eleven, Otto was not only a year older than his sister, he was a good deal stockier too. He hardly budged as she tried to work her way to the hoop.

When she reached a spot about eight feet from the basket, Jo suddenly reversed direction and put up a soft fall-away jumper. Although Otto had his hands up, he didn't come close to blocking the shot. The ball fell cleanly through the hoop, snapping the net back.

Jo's jersey was drenched in sweat. She'd already come from a full afternoon practice with the Branford Bulls, and going one-on-one against her brother in the Meyerson driveway was a workout in itself. Jo looked out at Otto from under her green baseball cap, which she wore backward, as usual. She had a satisfied half smile on her face, but she said nothing.

"Uh-oh, Miss Popularity thinks she's making a comeback—I can see it in her eyes," Otto said with a smirk. "But even after that stellar move, the Man still leads, nine to seven."

Jo looked at Otto quizzically. *What is this Miss Popularity stuff all about?* she wondered. She was used to being called Dime—a nickname she'd given herself because, she said, she was "ten times better than Penny Hardaway"—but Miss Popularity? He'd been repeating it the whole game.

Jo wished she were older and bigger than Otto. She hated when he acted superior—which was pretty much all the time. Otto was the top scorer on the Sampton Slashers, a team of ten- and eleven-year-olds that had beaten the Branford Bulls for the Danville County Basketball League championship two summers before.

Jo had been forced to try out for the Bulls, the Slashers' archrivals from the next town, because Otto and his obnoxious buddies wouldn't let a girl on their team. Jo, the best girl player in the fifth grade—and one of the best players, boy or girl, in the league—had made the Bulls as a starting guard. The Slashers and the Bulls had met again for the championship the summer before, and that time the Bulls had won.

Her brother acted as if she were

personally responsible for this humiliation. He just couldn't seem to beat her enough times on the Meyerson driveway to make up for it. *That's Otto,* Jo thought, *always thinking one-on-one*. The word *team* didn't mean much to him.

Since they were playing loser's ball out, it was now Otto's turn. He stood with the old, worn-down ball in his hands, about twenty-five feet away from the basket. "Give me this one?" he asked Jo.

"Sure, take it," she answered, backing off, pretending she wasn't playing defense. But at the last instant she leaped forward, trying to block her brother's shot.

Otto, as though he knew just what his sister had in mind, faked the shot, then drove around his off-balance defender for an easy layup.

"Schooled again!" Otto gloated, his usual obnoxious smirk on his pudgy face.

Man, he's annoying, Jo thought. She couldn't believe she'd fallen for the fake.

"That makes the score Otto the Great ten, Miss Popularity seven," Otto announced. "One more point and it's all over."

Jo didn't want to give in to her brother's teasing, but her curiosity got the best of her. "Okay," she said, readjusting her baseball cap and wiping the sweat from her face, "what's with this Miss Popularity business?"

"Well, you *are* the most popular kid on the Bulls, aren't you?" he asked, a cunning grin on his face.

"Um . . . ," Jo said hesitantly, her forehead wrinkled in thought. "Yeah, I guess they like me pretty much." She was suspicious now. She knew her brother too well to think he was simply complimenting her. Clearly he had something up his sleeve.

"Now why do you think that is?" Otto prodded, still with his mischievous grin. "You don't think it has anything to do with the way you give up the ball all the time, do you? You don't think it has anything to do with the way you just pass, pass, pass while Hopwood and Simmons and those other hotshots pad their scoring averages? You know, sort of the way Dennis Rodman does all the rebounding work, and Michael Jordan and Scottie Pippen get all the glory?"

Jo bit her lip. She didn't like what she was hearing. *Will Hopwood and Brian Simmons are my friends,* she thought. *They were the first two who accepted me when I tried out for the Bulls. Now Otto wants me to think they're using me. Well, I'm not even going to give him the satisfaction of getting into it with him.*

She checked the ball with Otto. "Ten-seven," she said. She wanted to get on with the game. "My ball out."

Jo dribbled in and gave Otto a few stutter steps. Sensing he was overplaying her to the right, she made a lightning move to her left, leaving her brother glued to his spot on the driveway. She scored easily.

"That makes it Burnt Toast ten, Miss Popularity eight," Jo crowed. "You never were much on defense, were you?"

Otto ignored the taunt. "Did you know that of all the Bulls' starters, you have the lowest scoring average?"

He's not going to let up on this subject easily, Jo realized.

"And how do you happen to know that?" Jo checked the ball for Otto. They continued to play while they talked. Otto missed a twelve-footer, and Jo rebounded.

REBOUND!

"Oh, I just happened to have a look at Big Jim's clipboard last week when you were playing at Harrison," he answered casually. He was referring to Jim Hopwood, one of the two teenage coaches of the Bulls. Jim was also a co-captain of Branford High's varsity basketball team. His younger brother, Will, was the Bulls' star center.

"Yup, you were right down there at the bottom. Numero five," Otto continued as Jo dribbled around the perimeter, pretending not to listen. "Roberts and Hopwood were at the top, just about even—although they're not quite up in my sixteen-points-a-game class. Then Simmons, then Danzig. And then . . . ," he said, trying to pinch her cheek, "my wittle sister, Jo Meyerson, Miss Popularity." He paused dramatically. *"Dead last."*

Jo cringed when she heard the words "dead last," and she swatted Otto's hand away from her face. Though she'd never really thought much about it, she wasn't surprised to hear that Derek Roberts and Will Hopwood were the Bulls' leading scorers. She'd figured that Brian Simmons, David Danzig, and she would be clustered right behind them. She'd never thought of herself as *dead last.*

She continued to dribble. "You know, scoring isn't everything, lame-brain," she said, trying to sound as though she didn't care if she *was* last. "I get just as much of a kick out of dishing the ball and shutting my man down on D as I do out of scoring."

Jo knew she didn't sound totally convincing. And the way Otto just kept smirking, as though he didn't believe a word she said, made her furious.

"Besides," she went on, "if I wanted to, I could outscore you anytime." Having said that, Jo dribbled in just inside the foul line, stopped, and popped.

"Ten-nine," she said, as if that settled the question.

Otto paid little attention to his sister's basket. "Oh, yeah?" he replied, absently checking the ball with Jo. "You can outscore me anytime? Why don't we see about that in two weeks, when the Bulls play the Slashers? We can play a little *mano-a-mano*—or is it *mano-a-girl-o?* Heh, heh," Otto chuckled annoyingly.

He emphasized his challenge by draining a long jumper over Jo's outstretched arm.

"Eleven-nine," Otto announced. "Game over. Miss Popularity *loses* for a change!"

He's so obnoxious! Jo found herself thinking for about the thousandth time. *It really* would *be great to outscore him in the Bulls-Slashers game, just to shut his mouth!*

As Otto opened the screen door to the kitchen, he added, "Well, the Slashers' top gun has had enough for today. I think I'll leave the Bulls' *role player* alone so she can work on her moves." He let the screen door slam behind him.

Jo was left alone out on the driveway, holding the smooth ball in her hands. She was the only girl on an all-boys team, and she knew one of the things they liked about her was her unselfish playing. And that was fine. She'd always played basketball that way—it just came naturally to her.

But she hadn't realized that *every* other Bulls starter was outscoring her. Wasn't she as good as they were? Was it possible that her teammates were taking advantage of her?

Jo pounded the ball on the pavement. She could hear the *thud* echoing in the quiet neighborhood. *Maybe I'm overdoing this team player business just a bit,* Jo thought.

Then, angrily, she drilled a twenty-footer.

"I hate to say it, but it's that time again," Nate said as he bent to pick up a basketball from the blacktop. Palming the ball in his huge right hand, he roared toward the basket closest to the gates of Jefferson Park for a thunderous dunk.

That's Nate, all right, Jo thought, *dunking in the middle of the Bulls' practice, for no particular reason—just*

because he feels like it. Nate Bowman, Jr., the Bulls' other coach besides Jim Hopwood, was widely considered the most outstanding high-school basketball player in Danville County. All the Bulls idolized him.

"What you're trying to say, Coach, is that it's time for us scrubs to be the bad guys, right?" MJ asked. Jo was constantly amazed that MJ could tell in advance exactly what the coaches had in mind. MJ's real name—incredibly—was Michael Jordan, and though he couldn't *play* anything like his namesake, he *knew* the game better than anyone on the team.

Every Thursday and Friday the Bulls' starters spent half their time at Jefferson Park practicing against their upcoming opponent. But since those opponents were from other towns and weren't really *there,* the Bulls did the next best thing: They scrimmaged against their subs and coaches, who *acted* like their opponents.

Jo didn't mind this routine, because she was a starter. But the subs weren't always so crazy about it.

"Hey, don't sweat it, MJ," Nate said soothingly. "At least we're not playing the Slashers, and you don't have to be Otto Meyerson." As soon as the words were out of his mouth, Nate shot a quick, anxious glance over at Jo. This kind of thing happened all the time: The Bulls were never sure if Jo would take offense when they were dumping on her brother. She just shrugged. *They don't need to worry,* Jo thought.

"Great," MJ responded sarcastically, "we don't have to be the Slashers. Instead, we get to be the Clifton Hawks. You know, the Slashers may be the most obnoxious team in the league, but the Hawks are a pretty close second."

Jo knew exactly what MJ meant. The Hawks did have some really nasty players. The two Jo remembered best were a guard called Skinny Sam and a power forward known as

Bulldog. In Jo's first game as a Bull the summer before, the two of them had talked trash to her from start to finish, just because she was a girl. They had even caused a minibrawl when they went out of their way to rough her up.

MJ stood facing Nate on the blacktop. "You're not going to make me be Skinny Sam, are you?" he pleaded.

Nate broke into his trademark wide smile. His gold stud earring gleamed in the late afternoon sun. "Nah, Skinny Sam's a guard. You may be skinny, but you're not a guard."

Then Nate beamed his mischievous grin at Mark Fisher, the Bulls' second-string backcourt man.

"Hey, no problem," Mark said with a smile as he wiped his prescription goggles on his shorts—something it seemed to Jo he did every time there was a break in the action. "I'll be Skinny Sam. Being annoying comes pretty naturally to me."

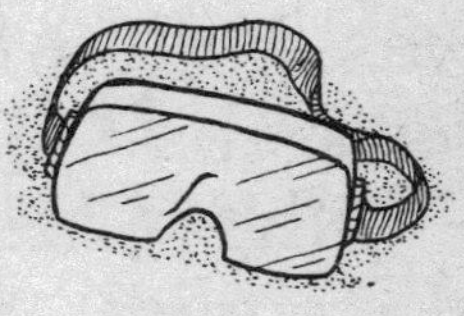

"You can say that again," Jim chimed in.

"Being annoying comes pretty naturally to me," Mark repeated with a wise-guy grin.

"How did I know he was going to say that?" Jo added. Mark considered himself the team clown, but Jo found a lot of his antics pretty predictable.

"Now wait a minute . . . ," Nate continued, his hand on his chin, as if he were thinking hard. "Aren't we missing a key player on the Hawks?"

Jo noticed Chunky Schwartz, the third of the Bulls' subs, tiptoeing off the blacktop toward the nearby trees as Nate spoke. Watching Chunky tiptoe was a hysterical sight, since he was built more like a whale than a basketball player.

"Oh, *Chunk*-y," Nate said in a singsongy voice. "We *need* you. *Some*body's got to be *Bull*dog."

"I *knew* it!" Chunky exclaimed, lumbering back to the blacktop. "Man, just like always. The subs do the dirty work, the starters get the glory."

Jo knew that Chunky's failed escape attempt and his huffiness over playing the role of Bulldog were all just an act. Chunky was the most easygoing kid on the team, and he could take a joke—as well as dish one out—with the best of them.

"Okay, enough talk. Let's play some hoops!" It was Dave Danzig, calling the team to action. Jo found this kind of funny, since Dave spent more time talking than anyone else on the Bulls.

Dave stood out on the blacktop halfway between the top of the key and the mid-court line. His blond hair fell in front of his eyes, and his baggy mesh shorts sagged down almost to his calves. He whipped the ball between his legs with such ease, it looked as though he could do it in his sleep. "Hey," he bragged, "I'm so good, why don't I be David Danzig?"

Jo couldn't believe he always used the same joke. But she had to admit, he *was* a pretty terrific dribbler. As a matter of fact, the two of them—Dave and Jo—were up there with the top ball handlers in the league. Together with Brian's shooting and the all-around play of Will and Derek, the Bulls were very, *very* difficult to beat.

Brian Simmons, an African American kid with a short fade haircut, watched Dave's show-off routine and shook his head. "I've got an idea," he said. "Let's try a *silent* scrimmage. See if Danzig can still dribble if he's not allowed to open his mouth."

Brian and Dave were next-door neighbors and best friends. Along with Will Hopwood, they'd been playing together since kindergarten. As a matter of fact, those three had started the Bulls.

Jim grabbed a ball and strode to the end line farthest from the entrance gates of Jefferson. He slapped his left palm against the ball, making a loud *thwack*. "All right," he announced, "me, Nate, Chunky, MJ, and Mark against the Bulls' starting five. Hawks' ball out."

Jim tossed the ball inbounds to Mark, who dribbled it up for the "Hawks." When Mark reached the front court, he passed the ball, sending it around the perimeter—to Jim, to MJ, then back to Mark.

The Bulls were playing a tightly packed two-one-two zone defense, designed to make a weak-shooting team such as the Hawks fire away from the outside. In this case it worked: Mark couldn't find a hole in the Bulls' D, and he hoisted up one of his long, one-hand, shotputlike heaves. Mark's shot wasn't pretty, but sometimes it surprised them.

This time, though, his shot hit the front of the rim.

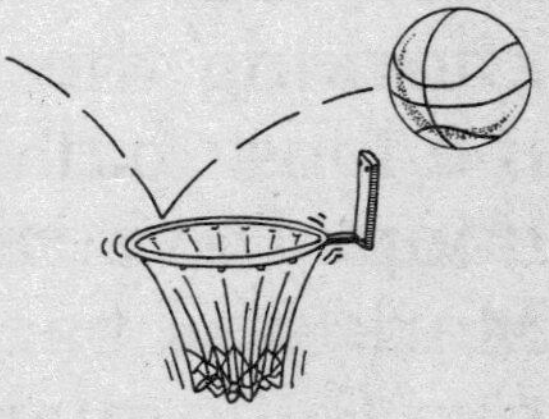

Will, the tallest of the Bulls at five feet four, hauled down the rebound and handed the ball off to Dave, who dribbled up to the Bulls' end of the blacktop. He put up three fingers.

Jo immediately realized this was a

set play for Brian. Like clockwork, Derek and Will came together to set a double screen along the lane under the basket. Brian ran behind the screen, lost MJ, who was guarding him, and put up a fadeaway jumper—his favorite shot.

Jo had to admit that the Bulls certainly knew how to run their offense.

Mark again brought the ball upcourt for the Hawks, but this time, just after he crossed the mid-court line, Dave flicked out his hand, knocking the ball away. Jo picked up the loose ball and broke for the Bulls' hoop. Dave ran along with her. Only Mark was back to defend against the two Bulls guards.

As Jo headed for the basket she saw Dave's hands extended, fingers spread, ready to receive the last-minute dish that Jo always made on a two-on-one fast break.

Not this time, Jo thought as she glided to the hoop and made the layup herself.

She and Dave dropped back to the other end of the blacktop. Jo noticed Dave looking at her with a puzzled expression on his face.

"Why risk an extra pass when I had the easy basket?" she said, feeling the need to defend her play.

"I suppose so," Dave answered, but he sounded unconvinced. Jo knew Dave well enough to sense that he was surprised and upset.

A few minutes later Dave and Jo were passing the ball back and forth at the top of the key, waiting for one of the Bulls' inside players to get free under the hoop. Brian shook loose from his defender in the left corner, his favorite spot. Jo saw him there.

But she didn't pass.

Instead, she launched a twenty-footer from above the top of the key.

The ball clanged off the back iron. The long rebound was pulled in by Chunky.

Hawks' ball.

As the Bulls again fell back on defense, Derek, who seldom said a word on the court, pointed out to Jo, "Brian was open."

Jo felt her face get hot. "I know," she snapped. "So was I."

Derek, a rail-thin African American kid who was the Bulls' top player, just raised his eyebrows. Jo knew that was about as much criticism as she was going to get from Derek. He preferred to just play his game and steer clear of the Bulls' squabbles. But she could tell he was upset by her failure to find the open man.

As the practice continued, the Bulls fell more and more out of sync. At one point the subs and coaches actually took the lead, something that almost never happened in these scrimmages.

Jo could tell that her teammates

and the coaches seemed confused and put out by her new style of play. At one point Will called for her to "see the floor," and another time Nate reminded her to "keep her head up"—both code phrases meaning she should have passed when instead she'd shot. But nobody seemed to want to confront her directly.

The way her teammates were reacting to her play made Jo uncomfortable. Being a member in good standing of the Bulls was the most important thing in her life. Still, Otto's words from the evening before echoed in her mind: *dead last, dead last, dead last . . .*

I'm as good a player as any of these guys, she kept thinking. *Why shouldn't I get in on the scoring fun?*

Nate pulled the Bowman's Market van—affectionately known as the Bullsmobile—into the parking lot alongside the Clifton Community Center, and the Bulls poured out. As usual, they were playing an away game, since the town of Branford had no community gym of its own. As they entered the building Jo braced herself for the trash talk she was sure to hear from Skinny Sam, Bulldog, and the rest of the Hawks. The Clifton gym

was one of the older, smaller ones in the league, and you could hear every sound echoing off the walls—from the fans in the bleachers as well as from the opposing team across the floor.

But as the Bulls filed by the Hawks, who were already warming up, she was surprised at the greeting: stares, yes, but silence. Obviously, Jo realized, the Hawks had been given a talking-to by their coach after the fight that had broken out the last time the two teams met. Although Skinny Sam *did* make a show of rolling his eyes when he saw Jo, as if to say, *They're still letting* her *play?*

Some guys'll never learn, Jo thought.

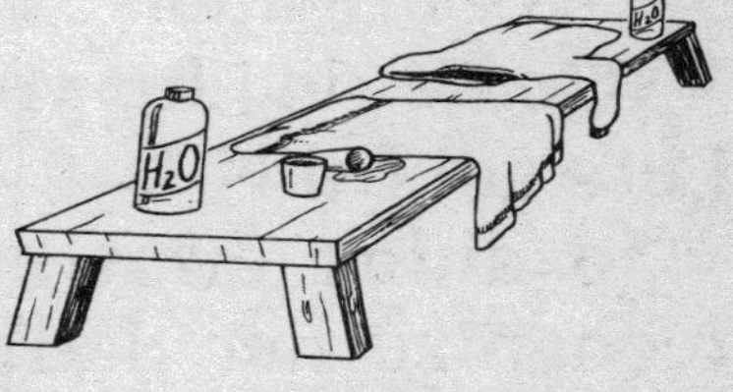

Jo and the rest of the Bulls ripped off their warm-up jackets and tossed them on the floor under the bench. Then they formed three lines for their weave drill. Jo felt butterflies in her stomach. She was always tremendously psyched before a game, but this time she didn't sense the same vibes from her teammates. Yes, the ball was moving briskly from player to player without ever touching the floor. Yes, there was the squeak of fast-moving sneakers on the polished wood surface. But their normal upbeat chatter and goofing around was missing from the Bulls' warm-up.

Jo had noticed the same thing in the Bullsmobile during the ride over from Branford. She wondered if the down mood was a carryover from the last practice, when she hadn't given up the ball as freely as she normally did. *Well, if it is, tough. Let someone else sacrifice for the team once in a while!*

"Come on, Jo, you're looking good! Let's go, Bulls!"

Jo didn't even have to look up to recognize her dad's encouraging bellow. *It's easy to figure out where Otto gets his loud voice,* she thought. The only difference was that her dad always meant well when he shouted, and Otto was . . . well, *Otto*. Still, it sometimes embarrassed her to hear her father's raucous cheering when the rest of the gym was quiet.

Jo scanned the bleachers, her eyes narrowed beneath her brown bangs. As she expected, she spotted Otto sitting as far away from their parents as he could get. *Typical Otto. He'll get a ride from Mom and Dad, but he thinks he's too cool to sit with them.*

A lot of people who didn't know the Meyersons well thought it was really nice that Otto came to all of Jo's games. But Jo knew better. Otto enjoyed nothing more than sitting in the stands and giving the Bulls the business—especially his "wittle sister."

Sure enough, as soon as their eyes met, Otto started in. "Gonna finally start taking it to the hole today?" he taunted. "Or is Miss Popularity going to keep piling up those assists?"

Jo just shook her head and blew her bangs out of her eyes. She wasn't going to let her brother distract her.

The buzzer sounded, signaling the end of warm-ups. The Bulls returned to their bench for last-minute instructions.

Jim stood in the middle of the huddle in his usual pose, arms folded in front of him. To Jo, Jim always looked real businesslike, while Nate seemed as though he'd rather be playing than coaching. Their coaching styles matched their personalities: Nate psyched up the team with his constant enthusiasm, while Jim took care of the *X*'s and *O*'s.

"Okay," Jim started, "you all know we beat the Hawks pretty soundly when we played them last summer. But they've got this new kid, Wilder MacCrae, from California. And from what I hear, he can really light 'em up from downtown."

Jo looked over at the Hawks' bench and saw the kid Jim was talking about. MacCrae was on the short side, very clean-cut, with hair so blond it was almost white. A real preppy-looking kid. "He doesn't look like anything so special," Jo whispered to Dave. He nodded.

"Also," Jim continued, "we looked a little raggedy in our last couple of practices. We need to move the ball better. We need to focus on D. Let's think pass. Let's play team ball."

It doesn't take a lot of imagination to figure out who this little lecture is directed at, Jo thought.

"All right, hands in," Nate boomed, putting his own huge hand in the middle of the circle. All the Bulls did the same. "Let's show these Hawks what's up. One, two, three—"

"Show time!" the Bulls shouted.

Will outleaped Jamal Wilkens, the Hawks' tall, bony center, on the opening tip, but Skinny Sam beat Dave to the ball. The Bulls fell back into a zone defense. Jim had told them they'd play zone and force the Hawks to gun from the outside, where they were weak. If this kid MacCrae was as good a shooter as people said, then maybe they'd switch to man-to-man.

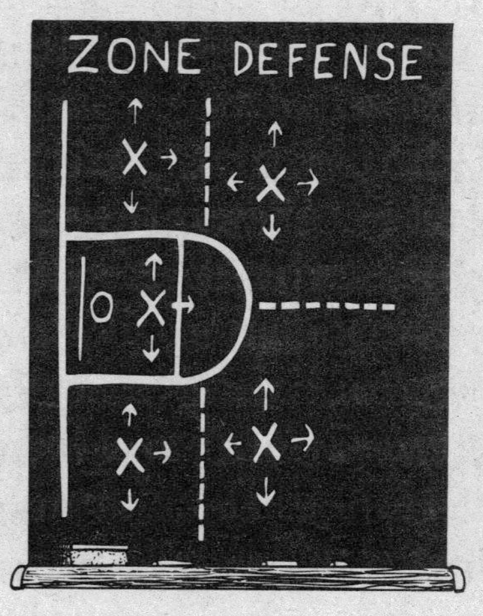

The Hawks rotated the ball around the perimeter. When it got into the hands of MacCrae, Jo played him real close, so she could challenge his shot. But the blond kid froze her with a ball fake, then drove around her. Before reaching the Bulls' inside defenders, he stopped and put up a soft eight-footer.

Not bad, Jo admitted to herself.

As Jo inbounded the ball after the basket, she heard Will call to her, "Let's think D."

Oh, as if you've *never been burned on defense before,* Jo thought angrily. But she didn't say anything.

Dave advanced the ball across the mid-court line and skidded a bounce pass to Jo. With barely a look at her teammates, Jo dribbled to the top of the key and launched a long one-hander. It rattled around the rim before falling in.

"Yes!" Jo cheered, pumping her arm.

"All right, sis, that's two!" she heard Otto shout. "Just fourteen more and you're in my class!"

How many times that week had she heard about Otto's sixteen-points-per-game scoring average? And that she was only averaging *six?* Well, there was one way to silence *that* kind of talk.

The next time the Bulls had the ball, Jo faked a pass to Derek, then drove by Wilder. She thought she was home free for the layup, but Bulldog came out of nowhere at the last instant to reject her shot. Skinny Sam wound up with the ball.

As the Bulls dropped back on defense Jo saw Dave and Will glancing at her, then at each other.

"What's the problem?" she asked them. "Is this the first time anyone on this team's ever had a shot blocked?"

Will just frowned back at her, shaking his head.

As they approached the midway point in the second quarter, with the Hawks ahead 20–16, Jim signaled for Dave to call time out. Though Jim was never a barrel of laughs on the sidelines the way Nate was, this time Jo could tell he was really upset.

"This isn't a team that should be beating us," he scolded, raising his voice. "We're getting no ball movement. The ball is in the hands of the guards too much. We need to work it in more."

Jo listened grudgingly, her arms folded in front of her. She knew when Jim said "guards," he meant her. But if he didn't have the guts to say it, she wasn't going to worry about it. Besides, why *shouldn't* it be in her hands? She could score as well as anyone on the team.

"Come on, Bulls," Jim encouraged, echoing his pregame message. "Defense. Ball movement. Pass."

"*Teamwork!*" Nate chanted.

But despite the pep talk from the coaches, nothing much changed. The Hawks' attack was a lot more explosive with Wilder MacCrae in the lineup than it had been in the past, and Bulldog was outmuscling Will and Derek in the paint. The Bulls' offense, on the other hand, was flat.

Jo reached double figures—on a wild, driving shot that gave her a total of ten points—with three minutes to go in the third quarter. But the Bulls were still behind, 32–27.

"We need a defensive stop!" she

heard Jim call out from the bench. "If we hold them and we score, we're right back in the game!"

Skinny Sam held the ball over his head at the top of the key. As Bulldog flashed through the lane Skinny Sam tried to hit him with a pass. But Derek, anticipating the play, stepped in front of Bulldog and picked off the pass. Almost instantly he flung the ball upcourt as Jo and Brian broke to the Bulls' hoop. Only Skinny Sam was back to defend.

Jo fielded Derek's pass cleanly and swept toward the basket. Skinny Sam, who'd been trying to stay between both Jo and Brian, had to choose one Bull to guard, and he picked Jo, leaving Brian wide open.

As Jo glided to the hoop she faked a dish to Brian—then kept the ball and scored the layup herself.

"All right, Meyerson!" she heard her dad explode.

TWO POINTS!

Make that twelve

points, Jo thought. As she was savoring her scoring output she caught sight of Brian glaring at her. Distracted, Jo got caught on a pick set by Jamal Wilkens, allowing MacCrae to swish an open ten-footer.

"Defense!" she heard Jim bellow angrily. "Come on, Bulls, *wake up!* It's time to turn it on!"

But the Bulls couldn't turn it on then, and they couldn't turn it on in the fourth quarter either. They lost to the Hawks, 50–43.

In the handshake line, out of sight of their coach, Skinny Sam and Bulldog were back to their obnoxious, wiseguy ways. "Upset of the young season, girlie," Skinny Sam gloated as he passed Jo.

Jo tried her best to ignore Skinny Sam. She saw her parents making their way carefully down the bleacher steps toward her.

Mrs. Meyerson put a consoling

hand on Jo's shoulder. "You Bulls'll get them next time," her mother said. "And Jo, what an *awesome* game you played!"

Otto too came sidling up to his sister. "Nineteen points—a career high for Miss Popularity," he announced. "But it was, after all, against the Hawks. Let's see what you can do against some *real* competition next week, when you play the Slashers."

Jo tried to ignore Otto as well. "Thanks, Mom, Dad. I'll see you guys back home," she said, attempting to smile. As she left the small Clifton gym for the Bullsmobile, she noticed that nobody seemed to want to walk with her. There were a lot of conversations going on, but she wasn't part of any of them.

She had a pretty good idea of what they were talking about, though. And when she heard Brian mutter to Will, "Since when did *she* become such a ball hog?" it left little doubt in her mind.

Ball hog! she thought. Jo felt the blood rushing to her face. Will had scored twenty-two points once in a game the previous summer, and Derek had notched twenty points two weeks later.

So how come nobody had called *them* ball hogs?

Jo was about to hop onto the empty stool next to Brian's, but Brian covered it with his hand.

"It's taken," he said flatly.

Jo looked at him, her forehead furrowed under her green baseball cap.

"I'm saving it for Chunky," Brian added, answering her questioning look.

Jo shrugged and headed for the stool next to Will's. But Will swiveled around on his seat and blocked her from that one too.

"MJ's sitting here," he announced.

So that's *how it's going to be,* Jo

thought. *And Brian and Will are two of my best friends on the team. . . .*

"Here, come on, sit with us," Dave called. Dave was sitting with Derek and Mark in a booth opposite the counter. He motioned for Jo to join them.

"It figures they have to bring in that MacCrae kid from out of state to beat us," Jo heard Mark saying as she slid onto the red vinyl-covered bench alongside Dave. This was part of the postgame ritual: drinking sodas at Bowman's Market and picking the other team apart. "Why can't anyone just play the Bulls without pulling that kind of stuff?"

"Not to mention the shoving and holding Bulldog was getting away with in the paint," Will added from the counter. "And that time Skinny Sam tripped Dave, and the refs didn't even call anything?" He smacked his forehead in disbelief.

"You call those guys *refs?*" Mark

continued. "They were just Hawks fans in striped shirts. I almost asked one of them if he wanted to borrow my goggles."

"Now why is it," Mr. Bowman asked from behind the counter, "that after every one of the Bulls' *infrequent* losses, I hear nothing but whining and excuses?" He was smiling, as he almost always did when he was talking to the Bulls.

Nathaniel Bowman, Sr., Nate's dad, was the owner of Bowman's Market. He was a balding African American man in his mid-fifties. With his stomach bulging slightly over his belt, you'd never know by looking at him that he'd once been an outstanding college player who was drafted by the New York Knicks. Unfortunately, he'd been injured before his NBA career ever got off the ground.

Mr. Bowman, a widower, lived for Nate's high-school games, and for the games played by the Branford Bulls. Since he had to mind the store on

Saturdays, he seldom was able to go to the Bulls' games—except the most important ones. But he loved to hear about every detail.

As Mr. Bowman kidded the Bulls about their excuse making, he began setting up cold cans of Pepsi on the counter.

"Pass me one of those?" Jo called out to her teammates on the counter stools.

"Yeah, sure," Brian said, "same way you passed me the ball on that fast break." He smirked at Will and made no move to hand Jo a soda.

Jo slid out of her booth. "*Excuse* me," she said as she reached between Brian and Will, getting her own Pepsi.

"So what really went wrong today?" Mr. Bowman pressed. His question wasn't directed at anyone in particular, but Jo looked down at her shoes.

"Our defense stank," Will said without hesitation. "And on offense we weren't getting the ball to our big men at all."

"Will's right—terrible passing," Brian chimed in. Then, looking at Jo, he added, "Make that *no* passing."

Oh, yeah? How many assists did you *get?* Jo felt like asking Brian, but she just bit her lip.

For a moment there was an awkward silence in the store.

"Hey, we weren't that bad," Dave said finally. "That new kid, Wilder, was pretty awesome. The Hawks played a good game—give them credit."

Dave glanced at Jo. As soon as their eyes met, though, he shifted his gaze down to the sodas on the table. She could tell by his expression that he thought the way Will and Brian were treating her was unfair.

What she really found puzzling was that when she'd first tried out for the Bulls, Will and Brian had been the ones who were willing to give her a fair chance, while it had been Dave who didn't want any girls on the team.

"What I'm gathering," Mr. Bowman said as he wiped the counter with a damp rag, "is that this wasn't the best game the Bulls ever played." Mr.

Bowman, as usual, was trying to make peace. It made him uncomfortable whenever any of the Bulls argued in his store.

Unfortunately, Jim wouldn't let the conversation die.

"There was just no team concept today," he said matter-of-factly.

"Bad chemistry," Nate agreed, nodding.

"No team concept," "bad chemistry"—what a bunch of wimps! Jo thought. *Why don't they just call me a ball hog to my face—the way Brian already did behind my back—and get it out in the open?*

Jo realized that her brother had been right. When she was delivering the ball to all the big scorers, everything was just fine. But now that she was starting to look for her own shots, all of a sudden she wasn't so popular anymore.

Jealousy, she thought. *Pure jealousy.*

"Thanks for the ride, Mom," Jo said as she slid across the seat and opened the car door.

Mrs. Meyerson nodded. "And remember, homework after practice," she reminded.

"I know," Jo replied. She gave her mom a wave and got out of the station wagon in front of the two stone pillars that marked the entrance to Jefferson Park.

A narrow paved path led to the blacktop court where the Bulls practiced. By habit, Jo dribbled while she

walked—behind her back, betw
legs. She was able to do this w
even thinking, which was a good th
because her mind was pretty busy.

Jo felt she was absolutely right in wanting to play a bigger part in the Bulls' scoring. Still, she was uncomfortable with the friction she was obviously causing on the team. Not the type to stew and keep things to herself for too long, Jo had discussed the problem with her mother on the drive over from Sampton.

Together they'd decided on a middle ground. She wouldn't return to being so totally unselfish that she felt the rest of the Bulls were taking advantage of her. But she wouldn't be a ball hog either.

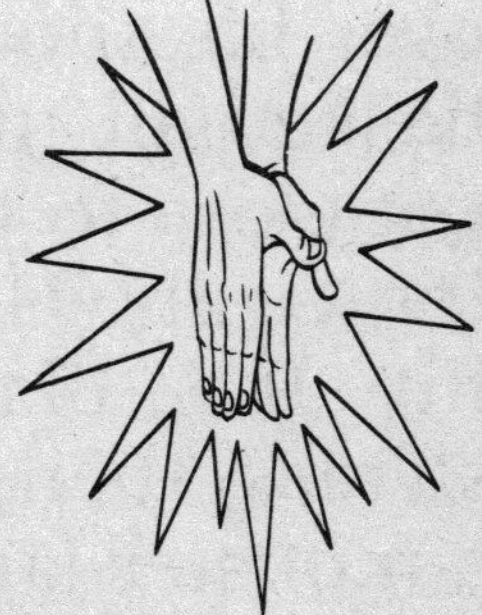

As Jo reached the blacktop Dave extended his hand for a low five greeting. Shaking his long blond hair out of his eyes, he smiled and said, "Just remember—whatever happens at practice today, you can still sit in my booth at Bowman's later."

Jo nodded. "Thanks," she said gratefully. Though she didn't anticipate any trouble that day, it never hurt to have an ally on the team.

"Hey, where are Jim and Nate?" Jo heard Mark asking as he worked on his thirty-footers. "They always bust our chops about being here early, and then they take their own sweet time."

At precisely that moment Jo looked up to see two tall teenagers in sweats and blue-and-white Branford High varsity jackets heading down the path to the blacktop. *If you've got to have coaches,* Jo thought, *the Bulls sure have the two coolest ones around.*

Jim carried the mesh ball bag slung over his shoulder, and Nate palmed a basketball in his right hand. As they got close to the court Nate began loping easily. He picked up steam as he hit the blacktop, took two huge strides, then soared above the rim for a monster jam.

Nice way to get our attention, Jo thought. Nate often called practice to order in just that way.

Though it was Nate who got the Bulls focused, it was Jim who started talking. That too was standard practice.

"Team," he began, "I don't need to tell you we haven't looked good in our last few practices, and especially in our game Saturday against Clifton."

Though most of the Bulls didn't look directly at Jim, Jo knew they were all paying attention. Maybe it was the dunks or the varsity jackets, but whenever Jim or Nate talked, the Bulls listened.

"We're going to get back to basics today," Jim continued. "Our passing game is what got us to the championship last summer, but lately our passing has been terrible. I'm going to have you try a drill we haven't done for quite some time. Let's get the starting five out on the floor to run your half-court offense against the subs and the coaches—but I want *five passes* before a shot is taken."

Jo felt her face get hot. They sure hadn't done that drill for quite some time. In fact, they'd *never* done it since she'd joined the team. That kind of forced passing was Mickey Mouse stuff. Maybe the Slashers needed that kind of discipline, but not the Bulls.

Jo could tell by the looks on the faces of the other starters that they were as unhappy as she was to be doing this drill.

"Come on, Coach," Dave complained, "you know that five-pass rule doesn't do squat."

One stern look from Jim, however, silenced any further protest.

Still, Jo knew just what Dave meant. Not only was the drill insulting, but it also led to some ridiculous situations on the court.

On the first possession, for instance, the Bulls' starters worked the ball around to Brian in the left corner—his sweet spot. But since they'd made only three passes, he had to give up the shot and kick the ball back out to Dave on the perimeter.

A few plays later Derek was slashing through the lane for what would have been an easy layup, but he was forced to dump the ball off to Will because they hadn't made five passes yet.

They worked on this drill for half an hour. Jo hated every minute of it. She couldn't stand stupid basketball, and to her, this was stupid basketball.

But what *really* hurt was that she knew exactly whom the drill was meant to help.

Jo had arrived at Jefferson resolved to play better team ball. But if this was the way the coaches were going to treat her . . . well, now she wasn't so sure.

Finally Jim and Nate called for a full-court scrimmage. Again, it was the Bulls' starters against the subs and the coaches.

Jo inbounded to Dave the first time the starters had the ball, and Dave hit Will with a bounce pass in the pivot. Jo cut through the lane, losing her defender on a pick set by Derek.

But Will didn't pass her the ball. He looked right at her—then passed instead to Brian in the corner. Brian drained a jumper.

Jo stared at Will. Will stared right back, a nasty half smile on his face.

On the starters' next possession, Jim called out, "Two!" This was a set play, and Jo quickly recognized that it was designed for her. As Dave triggered the play by passing to Brian, Will and Derek set a pick down along the lane on the right blocks. Jo dashed through the lane, found herself wide open behind the double screen, and waited for the pass from Brian.

It never came.

Instead, Will rolled toward the foul line, where Brian found him with a chest pass. Will took a turnaround jumper, but his shot fell short.

As the Bulls scrambled for the rebound Jo heard a piercing screech. Nate had blown the whistle. She could tell he was about to explode.

"You knew that play was for Jo!" Nate boomed, looking at Brian. "Why didn't you pass to her?"

"She wasn't open," Brian said with a shrug.

"Wasn't open, my you-know-what," Nate replied in disgust. "Hey, what do you think that whole drill was *about* before? Seeing the open man! Come on, guys, let's get with the program! What's going on here?"

Jo knew *exactly* what was going on here.

Brian and Will were freezing her out!

She couldn't believe it. After all those games when she'd led the Bulls in assists! *Man,* Jo thought, *for one game I concentrate on my own scoring, and what happens? The coaches hit the team with a rinky-dink five-pass requirement, and my "loyal" teammates freeze me out. Well, if* that's *how it's gonna be . . .*

When play resumed, MJ put up a shot from the corner for the subs, but he was off target. Jo grabbed the long rebound and started upcourt.

Without looking for anyone, she drove furiously through the second team's defense and scored on a wild layup over MJ's outstretched hands.

Coast to coast, Jo said to herself. *And that's only the beginning!*

For the next ten minutes Jo put up shots each time she got her hands on the ball. She took layups, jumpers, and running one-handers from every angle. Sometimes she was open, sometimes there were three defenders draped over her.

It didn't matter. She just kept shooting.

Out of the corner of her eye, she could see the two coaches. They both seemed to be getting angrier by the minute.

Finally, after Jo forced up a shot from way beyond the three-point line, she heard Jim scream, "Enough!"

The Bulls sat in the grass alongside the court. Jim and Nate stood on the edge of the blacktop, facing them. They both had their arms folded in front of them, and their eyes shone with fury.

Jo felt as if she were facing a firing squad.

"In all my years on this very playground," Jim seethed, "and in all my years playing for Branford High, I've never seen anything as childish and disgusting as what went on here this afternoon."

Jo wasn't sure if Jim's lecture was directed more at Will and Brian for their freeze-out or at her for her wild shooting spree. At this point, she didn't really care.

Jim looked slowly up and down the line of Bulls. "Anyone have anything to say?"

All the Bulls studied their sneakers or stared hard off into the trees. None of them wanted to make eye contact with Jim.

"All right," Jim concluded. "Practice tomorrow. Same time. Same place." Again he glowered down the line, looking at each of the Bulls. Finally he snapped, "There are a number of people on this team who are not playing Bulls basketball. I don't have to name names—you know who you are. All I can say is, it had better stop!"

He turned away to put the balls in the mesh bag. Without looking at the Bulls, he said over his shoulder, "Dismissed."

Jo grabbed her own ball and began dribbling back up the path toward the gate, where she was supposed to get picked up by her mother. Dave ran up beside her.

"Yo, Jo, the Essex Eagles are playing the Portsmouth Panthers in a makeup game in Essex tonight," Dave said. "My mom's going to give me a ride. Wanna go?"

"Why would you want to see the Eagles play the Panthers?" Jo asked.

"Well, I'd . . . uh . . . like to get a look at the Panthers' new point guard," Dave mumbled. "I don't want to go by myself—c'mon, go with me." Dave gave Jo a light punch on the arm. "Please?"

What the heck, Jo thought, *Dave's the only kid on the team still talking to me. I might as well go.*

"I'll have to ask my mom first," Jo said, giving in. "But I think she'll let me. What time should I be ready?"

"We'll be by your house at seven," Dave answered. With a smile, he added, “Just don’t bring Otto along.” He ran out the Jefferson Park gate through the stone pillars.

Jo shrugged and looked for her mother’s blue station wagon. She remembered how elated she had been the day she made the Bulls. There couldn’t have been a happier person in the state!

Man, she thought, *how did I ever manage to mess things up so bad?*

"Okay, you two," Mrs. Danzig said to Dave and Jo as she dropped them off at the curb in front of the Essex Community Center. "No hanging out after the game. I'll meet you right at this spot at eight-thirty."

"Right at this spot at eight-thirty," Dave repeated, snapping a salute to his mother. "Yes, ma'am!"

Jo laughed. Dave was such a goof. "Thanks for the ride," she called as Mrs. Danzig pulled away.

Jo and Dave figured they'd sit with the Panthers fans. It was always less crowded in the bleachers on the visitors' side. Jo picked her way to the top row. When she watched a game, she liked to sit as high up as she could. That way she could really see the patterns developing on the court.

Though she still wasn't entirely sure why Dave had been so hot to come to this game, she was kind of glad she'd tagged along. With all his joking and wisecracks, Dave was usually fun to be around. And it was nice to be away from the rest of the Bulls, considering the way they'd been treating her lately.

"The Panthers should win this one, no sweat," Jo commented as she watched the visitors, in their black-and-gray uniforms, go through their warm-up drills. The previous year Portsmouth had made it to the semifinals of the summer league before losing to the Bulls. Essex, as usual, hadn't even made it to the playoffs.

"Hey, don't count your chickens before they've hatched," Dave said, mimicking a line Mr. Bowman always used when he didn't want the Bulls to take something for granted. "Anytime you're playing against Sky Jones, you never know. . . ."

It was true that the Eagles' smooth forward could take a game into his own hands, and Jo knew it. She looked over to the home team's layup line and had no trouble finding number thirty-seven in the neon orange-and-green uniform of the Eagles.

Sky's physical appearance was imposing enough: He was tall and muscular, his dark brown skin glistened with sweat, and he had a lightning bolt shaved into his hair. But on top of all that, he didn't just walk, he *strutted*. He didn't stretch, he *posed,* as if there were newspaper photographers around to take his picture. Even the way he ripped off his warm-up jacket and dropped it on the floor demanded attention—as though he were an NBA star expecting some little towel boy to pick up after him.

Jo noticed that Sky never did anything

the simple way, but always the fancy, crowd-pleasing way. Even now, on the layup line, Sky wasn't content to dribble in and take a standard layup. He had to glide under the hoop and take a *reverse* layup.

There was no question that Sky Jones, along with the Bulls' own Derek Roberts, was one of the most talented players in the league. But while Derek got the job done quietly, Sky was just the opposite. Jo preferred Derek's way.

Early in the first quarter, with the score tied 4–4, Sky had the ball at the top of the key. With his defender all but smothering him, Sky still somehow managed to get off a twenty-foot shot. And made it!

"How could he miss seeing that guy in the corner?" Jo shrieked, jumping up from her seat. "He's got a teammate wide open, and he forces up a prayer like that? He's lucky he made it. Man, what a gunner!" She shook her head in amazement.

"The man likes to shoot the rock, no doubt about it," Dave agreed. Then he laughed. "I once kidded him about not playing defense. Know what he said to me?"

"No, what?" Jo asked.

"He said, 'Defense is something for my *teammates* to play,'" Dave answered. "The dude is a piece of work."

Jo and Dave continued to pick apart Sky and the rest of the Eagles and the Panthers. The Panthers' new point guard, the one Dave claimed he'd come to see, was a stocky but quick African American kid named Alfred Archibald. He was built low to the ground and was an excellent ball handler and tough defender, but his shooting was awful. Jo could understand why his teammates called him Air Ball.

But mainly they focused on Sky. Anyone who watched an Eagles game had to focus on Sky. Even though he was a forward, the ball seemed to be in his hands about ninety percent of the time.

Midway through the second quarter, with Portsmouth ahead 21–18, Sky was trapped in the corner by Dee Francis, the beanpole forward assigned to him, and by the two Portsmouth guards. Still, in spite of the triple-team, he forced up the shot. It fell way short of the basket.

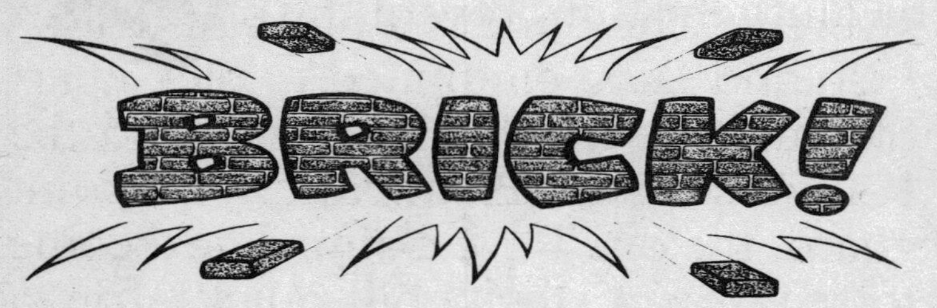

"Look at that!" Jo shouted, hitting herself on the head in disbelief. "Three guys draped over him, and he still shoots!"

As the game fell further and further out of reach for Essex, Sky tried to take over even more. In the closing seconds Sky was in the middle on a three-on-one break, with the two Eagles guards streaking down on the wings. The only Portsmouth defender back was a kid known as Bucky, a big center with protruding front teeth.

Bucky was forced to guard Sky, leaving the two guards wide open. But rather than give up the ball, Sky faked a pass to the guard on his left, hesitated, then tried to scoop in the layup himself. Bucky, however, timed his leap perfectly, and with a grunt he swatted the ball into the third row of the bleachers.

"Serves him right!" Jo cheered. She was on her feet. "What a ball hog! That's *disgusting!*"

She turned to Dave. He was staring at her, a half smile on his face.

Suddenly she got it. She felt as though she'd been kicked in the stomach. So *that* was why Dave had wanted her to come to this game!

"Dave," she began hesitantly, in a state of shock, "what Sky's been doing—is that the way I've been playing?"

Dave didn't answer her question directly. "According to my count, Sky has twenty-four points—but the Eagles lost, as usual," he said simply.

The realization sank in, and Jo felt more and more miserable. The way Sky had played, the way her brother Otto *always* played—to Jo, that was basketball at its worst. And the *last* thing Jo wanted was to be playing like her annoying brother!

As they made their way down the wooden bleachers, Dave put a hand on Jo's shoulder. "You know, you and I really play the same kind of game. Great ball handling. Great moves to the hoop."

Jo had to smile in spite of herself. No one could ever say Dave was lacking in self-confidence!

"And sometimes," Dave continued, "I get the itch to score a little more too—the way I think you've been itching lately. But we've got to distribute the ball—you know, keep the big guys happy." Dave gave Jo a light punch on the arm and smiled. "That's why they pay us the big bucks. And that's how we win ball games."

Jo thanked Dave and Mrs. Danzig and jumped out of the car. Then she ran up her front steps and pulled open the door to her house.

"Jo, it's almost nine o'clock," her mother said. Mrs. Meyerson was sitting at the kitchen table, reading the paper and waiting for Jo. "You've still got a little homework left to do."

"I know, I know," Jo replied, grabbing a banana from the fruit bowl on the counter.

"How was the game?" Mrs. Meyerson asked.

"Okay," Jo replied as she headed for her room. She had a lot on her mind and didn't feel like getting drawn into a long conversation.

"Yo, sis," she heard Otto call out as she passed the TV room. "Ol' Sky light it up as usual tonight?"

"Big-time," Jo answered. "He had twenty-four, but the Eagles still lost."

"Twenty-four points," Otto repeated slowly, impressed. "Man, you know something? You, me, and Sky could wind up as the three highest scorers in the league, if you keep shooting like you did against the Hawks."

Jo almost had to laugh. Sometimes her brother could be so *obvious*. He was still trying to sucker her into a shoot-out when the Bulls faced the Slashers over the weekend. He knew that would ruin the Bulls' balance, as it had against Clifton, and give the Slashers a better chance to win.

"Sure, Otto," she said, smiling to herself. "Me, you, and Sky . . ."

"Hey, Jo, things must really be tough when your own *parents* don't even root for you!"

That has *to be Matt Johnstone,* Jo figured. She looked over to where the Slashers were warming up at the other end of the long Sampton gym and saw she was right. It wasn't hard to pick Matt out of the crowd of black-and-gold jerseys. Even though he was short and skinny, you couldn't miss his bright red hair. He reminded Jo of a lit matchstick.

Matt was generally the one who

guarded Jo when the Slashers played the Bulls. And like the rest of the Slashers, he was totally into trash talk.

Jo had to smile, though, at his remark about her parents. In fact, they *were* sitting on the Sampton side of the gym. Jo knew how difficult they found it watching Sampton-Branford games, with their son playing for the Slashers and their daughter playing for the Bulls. The first time the two teams had played, Mr. Meyerson sat on the Branford side and Mrs. Meyerson sat with the Sampton rooters, but they'd felt silly splitting up like that. Since then, they'd tried sitting together and switching from one side to the other at halftime.

"At least she *has* parents," Dave shouted down to Matt. "She didn't crawl out from under a rock, like you." Dave could never resist a verbal battle—even if it didn't involve him directly.

"Whoa, sounds like Danzig's a little touchy today," Otto chimed in.

"Aw, he's just cranky 'cause the Bulls are on the road again," Spider McHale added, pushing his stringy dark hair behind his ears. "Like *always*." Spider played forward for the Slashers and was, along with Matt and Otto, one of their all-star trash talkers.

Man, at least they could try to think of some new lines, Jo thought. They were about as predictable as they were obnoxious. If it wasn't some diss about having a girl on the team, then it was a crack about the Bulls being the only team in the league without their own home gym.

Actually, Jo couldn't care less where they played. The truth was, she really enjoyed playing at Sampton's spanking new gym, with its full-size court and glass backboards. After all, the Bulls *had* won the championship on that very floor the previous summer.

Matt picked up where Spider left off.

"Nah, I don't think they're acting nasty because they're on the road again. I think they're a little *scared*. They know we crushed Winsted last week while they were losing to . . ." Matt hit himself on the head, pretending to try to jog his memory. "Wait, it wasn't the mighty Clifton Hawks you chumps lost to last Saturday, was it?" he asked sarcastically.

"Hey, listen to Carrothead talk the big talk because the Slashers are on a one-game winning streak," Brian called across the court to Matt. "Just check the standings after today's game. We'll be one and one and going *up*. You'll be one and one and going *down*." Brian squared up and calmly drained a jumper to emphasize his point. "Guaranteed," he added.

"Bulls, bring it in!" Jim commanded, putting an end to the war of words. He slammed a ball on the floor and looked as though he meant business. Jo knew that both coaches, but especially Jim, hated when the Bulls got dragged into these trash-talking sessions. But how could you avoid it with the Slashers? They were just so *obnoxious!*

"I've talked about focus with you guys at least a thousand times," Jim said angrily. "But I guess it hasn't sunk in yet. Now, *enough* of this baloney!"

All the Bulls looked down at their sneakers.

"Okay," Jim went on, "today we're going to play Bulls basketball. That means tough D. That means smart passing." Jim's eyes scanned all the Bulls as he talked. Then he fixed his glance on Jo. "That means *no selfishness*."

Although Jo's face grew hot, she couldn't really blame Jim for the reprimand. After her performance in the Clifton game, she knew she deserved the warning.

As Jim began to reach his hand into the circle of Bulls for a cheer, Jo took a deep breath and interrupted.

"Coach, just one thing . . ."

"Yeah?" Jim asked. He sounded wary.

"I'd like to try guarding Otto today."

There was a silence in the Bulls'

huddle. Jo saw Will and Brian exchange a knowing look.

"Listen, Jo," Nate jumped in. "You always take Matt. Droopy always takes Otto. That's the way we do it. Why would we want to switch now?" He rubbed his hand across his close-cropped hair. "I don't know if it makes a lot of sense for you to be guarding your brother. Things might get kind of, you know . . . *emotional.*"

Jo knew exactly what the coaches were thinking. She knew what Will and Brian were thinking, too. *They just figure I want to get into a shoot-out with my brother. They think I'm gonna go wild, like in the last game.*

Dave broke up the uncomfortable standoff. "Why don't we give Jo's idea a try?" he said. "I'd like a shot at Carrothead for once. And nobody knows Otto's moves like Jo. If it doesn't work, we'll switch back. No big deal."

Jim and Nate looked at each other. "Okay," Jim decided with a shrug. "We'll give it a shot."

Dave gave Jo a quick, secret wink.

"But if you guys get carried away," Jim continued, "if you and your brother get caught up in some all-Meyerson one-on-one competition, then forget it."

"In other words, if Otto gets it in his head that he's gonna score thirty points," Nate added, "you don't have to go and do the same."

Jo could tell that Will, Brian, and the rest of the Bulls were waiting for her to respond. But she just looked Jim and Nate in the eye and nodded at both of them.

The Slashers were already on the floor waiting. As usual, they were wise-cracking a mile a minute. The Bulls, in their red jerseys and dark blue shorts, walked out onto the court, each choosing a Slasher to guard.

Otto's eyes lit up when he saw Jo heading over to him. "All right," he said, delighted. "If it isn't my kid sister playing me! Hey, this is perfect. Now we can see which of us can get to twenty first."

Jo just shook her head slightly, barely looking at her brother. "Yeah, sure, Otto," she said.

The ref stood between Will and Ratso Renzulli, the Slashers' gawky center, and tossed the ball up to start the game. Somehow Ratso outleaped Will and tipped the ball over to Otto. But while Otto was surveying the court, before he even began dribbling, Jo's right hand flashed out and flicked the ball away from her brother. She recovered it herself and hurled a pass to Derek, who was streaking toward the Bulls' basket.

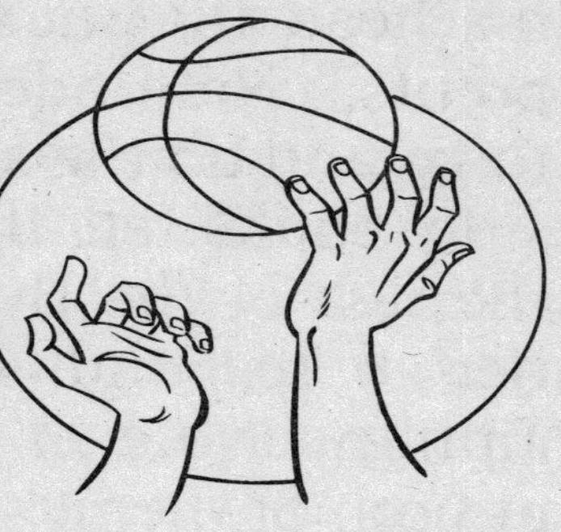

Easy layup.

Jo could see that Otto looked a little embarrassed as Matt inbounded the ball to him after Derek's basket, but he didn't say anything. As he dribbled upcourt in her direction, though, he *did* give Jo a pretty nasty look.

Otto advanced the ball to the top of the key. None of the other Slashers seemed to be moving. Jo had always noticed that the Slashers did an awful lot of standing around on offense, waiting for the player with the ball to go for the basket himself, one-on-one.

Which is exactly what Otto did. He tried a shake-and-bake move on Jo, hoping she'd buy the fake and think he was driving to the hoop. Then he stopped and went up for a jumper.

But Jo saw the move coming. She waited until Otto jumped, went up along with him, extended her right arm as far as she could reach, and blocked the shot.

"All *right!*" she heard Nate bellow from the bench. "I *love* this game!"

Dave retrieved the loose ball and began dribbling upcourt. Otto dropped back on defense. He still didn't say anything, but Jo could tell that he was no longer just embarrassed—he was *furious*.

Dave crossed the mid-court line and threw a bounce pass to Jo, who was on his right. Derek set a pick for Jo so that she was able to lose Otto and dribble to the foul line, where she squared up for an open fifteen-footer. But just before she released the shot, she spotted Brian cutting through the lane, and at the last second she hit him with a perfect two-hand over-the-head pass.

Brian made the layup, and the Bulls led 4–0.

As Brian loped back on defense he pointed to Jo. "Good look," he said to her, giving her credit for the pass.

"Way to move without the ball," she replied, returning the compliment.

Never mind the nineteen points I had against Clifton last week, Jo thought. This *is the way I like to play basketball!*

Throughout the rest of the first

quarter, Jo continued to smother Otto on defense. Not only did she prevent him from getting any open shots, but most of the time she prevented him from even getting the ball.

And on the other end of the court she was piling up so many assists that she heard Nate call out gleefully, "Move over, John Stockton. Here comes Jo Meyerson!"

As the opening quarter wound down, Jo could tell that Otto was winded. He wasn't used to working this hard to get open.

"Hey, Miss Popularity," he huffed, "back to your old ways? Playing the big D and dishin' the ball? What's the matter? Afraid your little Bulls friends won't like you anymore if you cut into their scoring? Tell you one thing, you're never gonna catch Sky Jones *this* way!"

"Maybe not," she answered her brother as she continued to shadow him wherever he went on the court. Then, under her breath, so he couldn't hear, she added, "But neither will you!"

With eighteen seconds remaining in the period, Brian alertly deflected a pass from Spider. Derek grabbed the loose ball and heaved it upcourt, where Jo was breaking for the basket, with Will trailing a few steps behind her. Not a single Slasher was back to guard against the fast break.

Jo caught Derek's pass cleanly and swept toward the hoop—but she didn't go in for the layup. Instead, she stopped short, sneakers screeching, and waited as Will came flying upcourt. Then she shoveled him the ball as he approached the basket. Will made the layup easily, extending the Bulls' lead to 15–9.

The entire Bulls bench—Mark, Chunky, and MJ, along with the two coaches—leaped to their feet, whooping it up over the resounding finish of the fast break.

"Sweet pass, Jo!" Nate screamed.

"Way to share the ball!" Jim added.

As Will hustled downcourt to play defense, he slapped Jo a low five.

"Looks like the *real* Jo is back," he said. "Nice dish!"

Jo smiled broadly. "Nothing to it," she answered.

"Mark, Chunky, MJ," Jim called out, looking around the huddle, "you guys are in. Go on, finish off those Slashers. Just be sure you know who you're guarding." To Dave, Will, and Derek, he added, "Take a rest. You did a great job."

Jo knew that Jim didn't really need to put Mark, Chunky, and MJ in the game in order to finish off the Slashers. With the Bulls carrying a 46–29 lead going into the last quarter, the coach just saw a good opportunity to give the subs some playing time in what had become a blowout. Jo herself wasn't worried about the Slashers getting back into the game with the lineup the Bulls now had out on the floor: She and Brian were still in there to anchor the team.

The Bulls' scoring pace cooled down slightly in the fourth quarter, although Jo still managed to hit a mid-range running one-hander as well as a finger roll after a gorgeous spin move. She also made sure she kept the defensive pressure on her brother red-hot. Jo liked the way Nate had described her tactics during halftime: "She's like those greenhead flies down at the beach," he'd said. "Bzzz, bzzz, bzzz—you keep slapping at them, but they keep coming back!"

Jim stayed with the same lineup the entire fourth period. When the buzzer sounded, the final score was Bulls 59, Slashers 43. It was

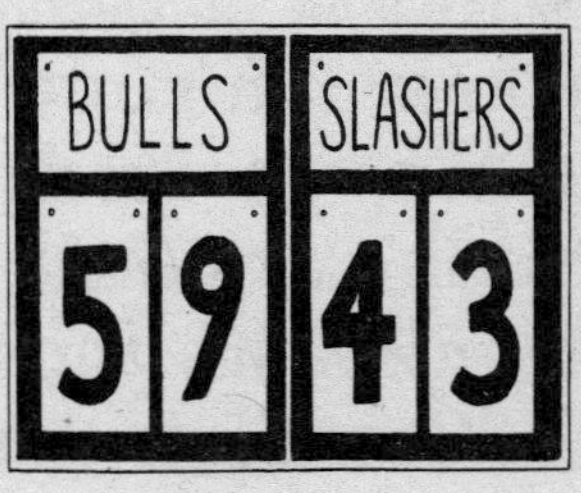

the most lopsided win in the history of the Bulls-Slashers rivalry. Jo wasn't surprised by the outcome: From midway through the first quarter, there'd never been much doubt about how the game would wind up.

Chunky lifted his pudgy arm in the air, index finger pointing skyward. "We're number one!" he chanted as he walked toward the Bulls' bench. "That's two in a row over those hotshots." He was referring to the past summer's championship game as well as this latest win.

"Face it," Mark added, "the Slashers are history. Make that *ancient* history."

"Hey, you think we could interrupt this celebration long enough to shake hands with those guys?" Nate asked. "That *is* generally what you do after you win a game."

"No problem," Brian replied. "I think we can be big enough to shake hands with those losers."

"Come on, let's act like gentlemen," Jim warned, turning on what the

Bulls referred to as his "authority" voice. "Just because the Slashers can be a little—"

"Obnoxious!" Will finished the sentence for him.

"Whatever," Jim said. "You know what I mean. Just don't sink to their level. Let's go over, shake hands, and get ready to go home."

Jo noticed that Jim left his clipboard with the score sheet on the bench when he headed over to shake hands with Mr. White, the Slashers' coach. She couldn't resist stealing a quick look before joining the handshake line.

You couldn't ask for much better balance than that, she thought, looking at the Bulls' point distribution:

Derek Roberts	15
Will Hopwood	12
Brian Simmons	9
Dave Danzig	8

Jo Meyerson	7
Mark Fisher	3
Chunky Schwartz	3
Michael Jordan	2
TOTAL	59

Jo noticed that she had fewer points than any of the other Bulls starters. Somehow it didn't bother her in the least. In fact, she felt absolutely great. She'd done her job and had been the best player she knew how to be—a *team* player.

The Bulls finished going through the postgame ritual with their rivals and were packing their gear into their gym bags when Jim stomped over to Jo and put his face inches from hers. For some reason he looked very angry.

"Meyerson!" he barked. "I thought I warned you about not getting into a scoring contest with your brother!"

Jo stared at her coach, dumbfounded. She hadn't given a single thought to scoring the entire game.

"W-What are you talking about?" Jo asked, her voice coming out in a broken squeak. She was stunned by the accusation. "I wasn't trying to outscore him. . . ." Confused, she looked down at the floor.

"Well, you *did!*" Jim continued. He slammed the clipboard with his free hand. "It says right here you outscored him—seven to three!"

The rest of the team burst into hysterics, but Jo stared at Jim, open-mouthed.

"Jo," Nate said, "he's *kidding*. Where's your sense of humor?"

Jo looked around the circle of Bulls and saw everybody laughing. Slowly a smile spread across her face.

"Oops," she said sheepishly. "I get it."

"I was just giving you a hard time because I can't *believe* you held Otto to only three points," Jim said, now grinning widely. "Here I was worried you'd come out firing away. Instead, what you did all afternoon was throw a blanket over that brother of yours! I've never seen *anyone* hold Otto down like that. That's about thirteen below his average."

"Tell me about it!" Jo laughed. "I only hear about his sixteen-points-a-game average at least once every waking hour—and sometimes even in my sleep!"

"Well, nobody ever called me a math whiz, but I'll bet you just knocked that average down a few points," Brian said. "Man, Jo, I never saw anything like the game you just played—and I've played some pretty good ones myself!" All of a sudden Brian looked down toward the other end of the gym. "Hey, what's going on over there?"

There was a commotion around the Slashers' bench. It almost sounded as though a fight had broken out. From what the Bulls could hear, Coach White really seemed to be bawling out the Slashers—and the players seemed to be giving it to each other.

"You boys were the pits today!" they heard Mr. White yelling. "You embarrassed the heck out of me. I never thought I'd see the day when the Slashers would lose to the Bulls by sixteen points on our home court!"

"Yeah, well, if Matt had ever gotten me the stupid ball instead of showing off his dribbling skills all day, things might have turned out a little differently!" Otto shouted.

"Oh, Meyerson, gimme a break," Matt shot back. "You just can't handle getting shut down by your little sister."

The Bulls, who had been listening to all of this, broke out into loud laughter at this point.

"One thing you can say about those Slashers," Mark choked out, "they're such good sports."

"You're right," Will added sarcastically, "they really take losing well." Then he turned to Jo. "Hey, I was wondering. After that nineteen-point explosion against the Hawks last week, and playing head-to-head against your annoying brother—weren't you tempted to take it to the hoop more than you did?" he asked.

"Nah," Jo answered, "I'll leave that trigger-happy stuff to Sky Jones—and to Otto."

She put an arm around Dave's shoulders and gave him a knowing look. "Us guards, we'd rather just distribute the ball and keep you big guys happy. That's why they pay us the big bucks!"

Don't miss Super Hoops #9,

Hang Time, coming soon!

"Well, guys," Mr. Earl asked, "what do you think of our faculty team?"

Dave threw himself to the ground, pretending to pass out. "Mr. Earl, no offense," he finally replied. "But you call the group of klutzes you just had out on the floor a team?"

Mr. Earl smiled patiently. "I was thinking about what Brian was saying to me the other day—about the Bulls being able to crush the teachers in a game. So I invited a few of my faculty friends. I suppose we could use a little more practice. But if you really think you can take us, we're up for it." Mr. Earl looked directly at Brian as he issued the challenge.

Brian thought about how easy it would be to steal the ball from Ms. Darling. How much fun it would be to go head to head with Mr. Earl. Of course, Mr. O'Shea would also be playing. . . .

"You want us, you got us!" Brian heard Will bellow.

About the Author

Hank Herman is a writer and newspaper columnist who lives in Connecticut with his wife, Carol, and their three sons, Matt, Greg, and Robby.

His column, "The Home Team," appears in the *Westport News*. It's about kids, sports, and life in the suburbs.

Although Mr. Herman was formerly the editor in chief of *Health* magazine, he now writes mostly about sports. At one time, he was a tennis teacher, and he has also run the New York City Marathon. He coaches kids' basketball every winter and Little League baseball every spring.

He runs, bicycles, skis, kayaks, and plays tennis and basketball on a regular basis. Mr. Herman admits that he probably spends about as much time playing, coaching, and following sports as he does writing.

Of all sports, basketball is his favorite.